Shadow of the

Shadow of the Wild Hare

MARGUERITE POLAND

ILLUSTRATED BY LEIGH VOIGT

DAVID PHILIP

CAPE TOWN   JOHANNESBURG

The author and illustrator wish to express grateful acknowledgements to the staff of the Mammal Research Institute, University of Pretoria, for their assistance with information about the *pondhaas*, or riverine rabbit, and to Mr P J van Rensburg, whose photographs were used for reference.

A note by the author on the riverine rabbit is to be found on page 86.

SECOND IMPRESSION 1988
THIRD IMPRESSION 1989

First published in 1986 by David Philip, Publisher (Pty) Ltd,
P O Box 408, Claremont, Cape, South Africa
© text Marguerite Poland 1986
© illustrations Leigh Voigt 1986
ISBN 0 86486 073 0
Printed and bound in South Africa by Creda Press,
Solan Rd, Cape Town

FOR THE ROSSES OF GRAHAMSTOWN AND
THE PRINGLES OF 'FAIR HOLT'
WITH MUCH LOVE

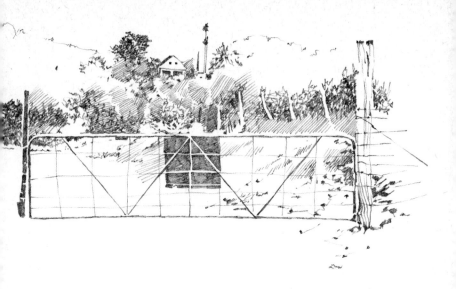

1

Dan asked Rosie to play shop with him through the pantry window as Grandma did when she came over from the big house to visit. Nomatse's sons wanted to play too. They stood behind Dan with dusty feet and gazed at Rosie like a little flock of rock-martins perched together. So Rosie went to the pantry, opened the shutter and leant out.

'Yes, Dan? Can I help you?' she said.

'Rosie!' cried Dan. 'Not like that! You must be a shop-person, like Grandma!'

Rosie laughed, remembering how Grandma always acted when she played the game. She squinted her eyes and screwed up her mouth so that Nomatse's little boys drew together, ready to run.

Dan collected some sweaty stones for money. He slipped them over the sill and squealed when Rosie leant too close. She hooked her fingers and glared at him just as Grandma used to do, so that Rosie – when she was very small – had only half-believed she was Grandma and not mad Tant Jacoba Pandoer, who lived in the roadworkers' houses near Kareebos.

Rosie opened the sugar bin and the children came to the window, nudging at each other like little goat kids. They held out their palms to be filled.

Rosie gave out sugar and biltong, rusks and raisins for payment in peach pips and stones. She sold a mug of grain to Sipho to feed to the bantams and cut Dan some beetroot tops for the white rabbits, that lived in the pen next to the orphaned lamb. She bartered jelly-powder for green loquats and grumbled all the time in a querulous voice.

Rosie peered into each of the tins on the shelves searching for a sweet for herself but all she could find were packets of gelatine and soup. It was rare to discover a toffee or humbug that her younger brothers Skip or Dan had not found first. It was only near Christmas that the boxes and jars were full of things to eat and the big festive fruit cake sat, an inch deep in hard white icing, looking rather surprised at itself under the wire dome that kept off the flies.

Skip came to the pantry window, followed by his friend Willie Tromp from the neighbouring farm. They pushed their wire-cars over the brickwork and watched Rosie counting out peanuts for Dan.

'Give us a rusk, Tannie Pandoer,' said Skip, grinning.

2

'Where's your money?' asked Rosie, tilting her head and looking at him sideways out of one eye. Skip gave her a handful of loquats. 'I'll cut some biltong if you'll take a dish of pellets to the rabbits,' she said, in a high, sharp voice that she hoped might sound like Jacoba Pandoer's.

'No, man,' interrupted Willie. 'We're going to swim in the reservoir behind your Ouma's house. Give me the biltong,' and he snatched the stick from her and ran off.

'Shop's closed now,' said Rosie, throwing a loquat after him and missing.

'Ah no!' cried little Dan. 'Me and Sipho want you to be that funny shop-person still.'

'Got to go and feed my turkeys,' she said, remembering that Jacoba Pandoer kept turkeys in her backyard. She offered Dan and his friends a half-finished tin of condensed milk to eat and they raced away to the front to Oukan, the old deaf-mute man who worked in Grandma's garden, to beg for a ride in his wheelbarrow. When they had gone Rosie filled one of Dan's baby bottles with milk and took it to the lamb whose mother had been killed by a jackal the week before. She scratched at its bony little forehead and rubbed its woolly neck, while Skip's pet crow watched from its perch.

The yard was very still. The only sound was the noisy sucking of the lamb. But suddenly something made Rosie turn, startled. It seemed as though even the cicadas had stopped their shouting to watch.

There was a man standing by the kraal-wall. He

carried a bag slung over his shoulder. He wore a coat which hung about him like a loose, black hide. A jackal's tail was wound around his head. Rosie drew in her breath, afraid he might have seen her squatting by the pen. But he did not move. He stood quite still and waited.

Rosie did not need to ask him who he was. She knew. She had often heard her father talk of him. He was Tantyi Mayekiso, the jackal-trapper.

Quietly, Rosie went on bare feet down towards the house. Her *hanslammetjie* called after her. Skip's crow set up a clatter but Rosie ran as fast as she could, not looking back.

She went through the hall calling softly to her father, in case – even from so far outside – the trapper could have heard.

Her father had just come in from the lands and Rosie said, all in a rush, 'The trapper's here! He's waiting in the yard.'

'Oh good,' said her father, as though nothing strange had happened. 'Tell him I'll be up in a minute.' But Rosie hesitated, not wanting to go alone and her father said, 'What's wrong, Rosie?'

Rosie shook her head. 'Nothing,' she replied and she went away because she did not want him to know she was afraid. She walked slowly round the side of the house, past the kitchen and the washing and the quince hedge and, hanging in a tree, the old iron pipe which was used as a gong.

The shed doors were closed, the workshop was empty and Tantyi Mayekiso sat beside the kraal-wall.

He was so still Rosie would not have seen him if she had not known to look. She went towards him. She could barely hear her own footfall but the trapper turned his head long before she reached him as if he'd listened to each step.

'*Uyez 'ngoku,*' she said, almost in a whisper. 'He is coming now.'

The trapper nodded slightly – just a tilt of the head – and Rosie hurried off to find Skip, thinking of the strange slant of the trapper's eyes and the tips of his jackal-tail hat catching drops of sunlight.

Skip and Willie were swimming in the reservoir.

'Skip,' called Rosie, 'Skip!' But he did not hear because Willie Tromp was trying to duck him and was shouting and splashing like a *kapater* in a dip.

'Skip! The trapper's here!'

Skip popped up and stared at her, suddenly still.

'The trapper?'

Rosie nodded. 'He's come back.'

Skip whistled between his teeth. He did it all the time since Willie Tromp had showed him how. 'Hey, Willie! The trapper's here!'

Willie sniffed in the loud piggy way that always made Rosie cross and said, 'My Pa says that the jackal-catcher sucks blood. In the night. Anytime he can find something to suck it from.'

Rosie looked impatient. 'Do you want to see him?'

'Of course,' said Skip. 'He might swop some pelts.' He pulled himself up onto the reservoir wall next to Willie. They jumped down and hurried off towards the yard.

6

Tantyi Mayekiso was a young man. His movements were slow, quiet, as though he chose his time to move – as a bushbuck does, from light to shade to light, so that it is not easily seen.

He watched the boys come closer. Even Skip – Rosie could see by the way he stood – was a little afraid as he asked the trapper to show what he kept in his bag. Only Willie Tromp seemed unconcerned. He was still rubbing his nose and flapping at flies with his big loose hands.

The trapper would not open his bag for Skip nor answer any of the questions that he asked, so Skip retreated to the kraal-wall with Willie and pretended not to stare as they took turns to balance upright on the gate.

At last their father came, and when he walked across to the trapper and said, '*Molo*, Mayekiso' in a voice no different from the way it always was, things seemed right again to Rosie. And because the silence of the yard had been driven away, Rosie ran back to the house and told her mother and little Dan – off-hand as though it happened every day – that the trapper had come to catch the jackals and the *rooikatte* that had been killing the sheep and goats.

When Rosie returned to the yard the trapper had gone and Skip and Willie were water-bombing the mice that lived in the thick creepers growing up the kitchen wall. She went back to the rabbits and sat on the ground outside the pen, allowing the lamb to suck at her fingers. She listened to the slow sounds of the afternoon settling in again: the windmill turning by the

7

reservoir, the rush and sweep of wings as her mother's fantailed pigeons took flight, the rattle of Oukan's barrow as he pushed it along the gravel path to the big house where Grandma lived.

She stayed in the yard, not daring to go beyond the gate that led out into the road. For there, she knew, she would find the trapper's footprints in the sand where he had left them when he walked away. Beyond the cattle-grid the veld lay hot and still, as though the afternoon waited with its eyes half-closed.

Evening came. Swifts and swallows hawked above the dam and Willie Tromp mounted his old bike and rode home. The cows were brought in to the kraal and Rosie ran down to the shed to watch the milking. The dairy was busy and Ratbag the sheepdog stood at the gate and barked at people coming back from the store at the drift. The voices of the goats carried across the camps and the old electric generator started up with a slow, homely took-took-took.

At supper Rosie's mother spooned vegetables onto the plates while her father carved the meat. He said,'Did you hear that the trapper came, pet? Strange fellow – he didn't want more than a bag of mealie-meal and some salt. I sent him over to Kareebos where we've had all that trouble with jackals.'

'I wonder how long he'll stay?' said Rosie's mother as she poured milk into Dan's glass and wiped his face.

'Depends on how quickly he gets rid of them.'

'How does he trap them, Dad?' asked Skip.

'I don't know. He seems to spirit them away in the night. But once he's been, there are no more jackals for

8

a while. Sometimes its better not to ask.'

'I wanted to know what he kept in his bag, but he wouldn't tell me.'

'I should think it's full of weird potions. He must collect all sorts of things in the veld. He's half wild himself. I'll swear he thinks like a jackal.'

Skip and Rosie glanced at each other. 'Willie Tromp says he sucks blood, 'said Skip. 'Willie Tromp says he turns into a jackal when it's dark and tricks the other jackals.'

'What sucks blood?' said Dan, peering over the edge of the table, his mouth full of potato.

'The trapper.'

'What's a trapper?'

'Of course he doesn't suck blood!' said their mother soothingly. She frowned at Skip and shook her head.

'What's a trapper?' insisted Dan.

'Eat your supper, Dannie,' said Rosie, coaxing him with a spoonful of gravy and mash. Dan pushed it away crossly and said, 'What sucks blood? What person is that?' and would not be satisfied until Rosie promised to give him one of her bantam chicks.

After supper, while their mother was putting Dan to bed, Rosie followed Skip to his room. She sat on the floor and watched him as he polished up the wire-car that Oukan had made for him. It was a Scotch-cart drawn by two horses. Their legs moved forward and back in perfect rhythm. The cart had a little metal seat and three wide rubber-trimmed wheels. It smelled wonderfully of the tractor shed, of iron and oil.

Skip's room was full of hunting trophies – buck

9

horns, pelts and skulls. The clothes in the open cupboard were bundled into the back to make way for more important things – a box of ammunition for his rifle, a hunting-knife, a toffee-tin of marbles.

Rosie lifted down the box of marbles and looked inside, choosing her favourites. She rubbed the little rust spots off an ironie and held it in her hand, testing its weight.

'What do you think the trapper is doing now?' said Skip suddenly.

Rosie hugged her knees and curled her toes under for a moment. 'I don't know.' She did not wish to speak about him.

'Willie says . . .' began Skip.

'What does Willie know!' retorted Rosie.

'Well, Dad tried everything to get rid of the jackals and he never got anywhere. The trapper must have some kind of special *muti* . . .'

Rosie went away then because it was already dark outside and she did not want to think of Tantyi Mayekiso. She got into bed and read a book about horses and gymkhanas and English girls who were stable-hands and she fell asleep long before her father switched off the light-generator.

She did not know what time it was when she awoke. There was no way of telling because it was dark except for a half-moon shining up above the ridge. She lay listening, for she had heard a sound – somewhere in her sleep – far, far outside, like the cry of a jackal, ringing out among the stones of the hills beyond the house.

She lay with the blanket pulled up to her chin, imagining the ridge with the half-moon shining on it. The sheltered slopes were covered with wild olives, sneezewoods and gwarri. There was an *msenge* tree and an ancient *witgat* near the trough, where springbok often came to drink. Beyond it was Kareebos, the deserted grazing-farm where her father ran extra flocks of goats.

It was from that ridge, Rosie knew, that the sound had come – one jackal voice calling to another. And it was on that ridge, way up at the crest where a huge rock was cleft in two, that once, a hundred years before, a diviner had fallen to his death. His shade, people said, lived there still, restless and alone.

Rosie got out of bed and crept through to Skip's room. He was asleep and only mumbled and turned over when she shook him. She took the kaross from the end of the bed and wrapped it around herself, willing Skip to wake. She sat in the chair by the window. The curtains were open. She could see the Southern Cross dipping low above the hills. Like a tall giraffe it seemed to lean across the sky.

On the window a baboon skull brooded. Rosie buried her face in the kaross to block it out. Again, far away in the night, a jackal yelped and Rosie knew that within the dark and moving stealthily along some deep ravine, the trapper Tantyi Mayekiso, was hunting out the jackals, jackal-like himself.

2

When Rosie awoke the next morning she was still sitting in the chair in Skip's room. Dan was riding his scooter up and down the passage making motorbike noises as loudly as he could, but Skip's bed was empty and Rosie knew he would be out in the milking-kraal with their father.

She dressed and went to the kitchen. Nomatse was singing hymns while she made breakfast and Dan's pet chicken bobbed up and down at the flyscreen, anxious to get out. Rosie opened the door so it could escape and pinched the corner of the crust from the loaf that Nomatse had just taken from the oven. Somewhere in the yard someone thumped at the iron rod strung in the tree, calling the workers to eat.

Rosie took food to the orphan lamb. The crow watched from its perch, tilting its head this way and that, and snapping its beak. She stroked the white rabbits and talked to them in a soft sing-song voice. She looked up as Skip climbed over the yard gate and came across to squat beside her.

'I heard Ma say she's taking Dan and Grandma to town to visit Auntie Dorcas this morning,' he said. 'Are you going?'

'Are you?'

'Don't be mad!' he said and Rosie laughed. Auntie Dorcas's house smelt of dusty ferns in baskets, and the fox-terrier with bright yellow eyes always nipped at their heels in a sneaky way. Auntie Dorcas boiled milk for the tea and served all children with thick slices of bread and fish-paste. Rosie and Skip had buried more fish-paste sandwiches in the quince hedge than they could remember.

'I'm riding down to Willie's,' said Skip. 'He wants me to go hunting with him.'

'And Dad?'

'He said that he was dipping at Kareebos.'

Rosie felt alarmed. If she stayed behind there would only be Nomatse in the house and perhaps, while the others were away, the trapper would appear as suddenly as he had the day before and stand there in the yard, watching with his strange, dark, slanted eyes. She left the lamb and Skip and ran off to find her father to ask if she could go with him and watch him dip the goats.

'You can come if you promise to make me a decent

14

tea, Rosie!' he said. 'Bring biltong, rusks and some sandwiches!'

'Fish-paste?'

Rosie's father grinned. 'No thanks, Auntie Dorcas! I had my fill of those when I was small!'

They set out after breakfast, the bag of rusks on the seat between them. Rosie gnawed at some biltong and chatted to her father about dipping and lambing, goats and bantams. She jumped down from the truck each time they stopped at a gate, glad she could open them without arguing with Skip about which were his and which were hers.

Rosie loved gates. Each had a personality of its own. There were friendly gates, like the one at the home dam that swung down into long grass and sometimes got marooned in rainy weather, and gates that nestled among thickets of bush, pointing the way along exciting paths. There were gates that stood alone in the open veld and in whose wires the wind strummed mournfully, and old familiar gates like those set in the ironstone walls of the goat-pens. But if some gates were friendly, others were not. They were reluctant to unfasten and let her through and sometimes they pinched her fingers spitefully as a warning not to come too often, as though the secrets of the bush beyond were something that they did not wish to share.

Rosie's father took the district road that passed the siding and the row of road-workers houses where the big yellow bulldozer and the grader were kept in a shed. Rosie looked back to see if she could see mad

Tant Jacoba Pandoer in her yard with her turkeys, but only Oom Poen, her brother, was standing at the fence to see them driving by. They turned the corner and took the lonely track leading to Kareebos, where Rosie's father ran his flocks of goats for extra grazing.

Rosie's father parked the truck under a sweet-thorn near the pens where the goats had been waiting since early morning. Rosie climbed out and went to sit on the wall near the dip. She watched the kids and *kapaters* mill around, sending up the dust.

After a while she went to explore by herself. She scuffed the sand with her toes, looking for the bits of broken china that could always be found where once the rubbish heap had been.

It was very quiet. There was no wind to stir the grass. The silence lay waiting among the sheds and outbuildings. Here, no men went about their work in twos or threes, no children trundled tyres down the road, guided with a stick. Here, even the birds were different. They hid in the thorny shade and watched with small dark eyes and fierce hooked beaks to see who passed. There seemed to be no buntings piping or *dagbrekertjies* calling in the new morning. Here were *jiza* birds and jackie-hangers that flew up suddenly, leaving hoppers dangling from a thorn.

Rosie wandered down to the old shed. It was shadowy inside – a dusty-blue darkness, undisturbed by people. She stood in the doorway, very still, as though waiting for the gloom to go so she could see the floor and the forgotten bales of straw and the broken rakes and ploughs. She sniffed at the smell of old goat-droppings, tractor grease and sacks.

There was a movement in the corner – small, so small she hardly saw it. She went forward, searching with her eyes. There, ears flat against its back, was a hare. It crouched low. Its breath came so fast and short it seemed to tremble rather than to breathe. Its eyes were closed to slits.

Rosie crept closer. The hare did not move. She knelt beside it but it strained away from her – a savage, wild little thing. And then she saw that its foot was tethered to the food-trough with a thong. It could not move. It could not run away.

Rosie looked around to find something with which she could cut it free and as she looked she noticed that flung across the old wooden baler were skins of a jackal and a *rooikat*. They hung with strange, small vacant spaces where the eyes had been but as though, from the shadows of the shed, they watched her still.

Rosie sprang up, almost starting for the door. She had discovered the trapper's lair, the place where he kept his pelts. Surely he himself was hiding in the rafters, like a *rooikat* on a rock, waiting to pounce. She looked up, but the beams were bare except for the place where they rested on the top of the wall and a pair of sparrows sat side by side in the shelter of the eaves.

Hastily Rosie undid the thong from the food-trough and picked up the hare. It kicked and struggled as she put it in one of the empty sacks that lay on the floor. She went across the yard and climbed through the fence to the pens by the dip.

'Dad,' she said breathlessly, 'I found a little hare tied

up in the shed.'

Her father looked over at her. 'Tied up?'

Rosie nodded. 'It was fastened to the food-trough with an old piece of rope. Also, I saw a jackal- and a *rooikat*-skin in there.'

'That must be where the trapper's keeping his pelts dry,' said her father, as he pushed a goat under the water until only its nose showed.

'Why'd he have to catch a hare?' Rosie was indignant.

'He's got to eat, pet,' said her father matter-of-factly.

A goat had lost a horn as the stockman tipped it into the trough. Bright blood oozed down onto its neck and through its hair. Rosie turned away, not wanting to see. She took the sack to the truck and laid it on the floor. No one was going to eat the hare. No one. She would put it with the rabbits and make it tame. She would feed it like her lamb or Skip's crow and then she'd build a bigger pen with a little run in front and ask old Oukan to help her find a mate for it.

Jacoba Pandoer's brother's house was the first of three built near the siding where the roadworkers lived. There was a windmill, a reservoir by the fence and a huge sunflower growing just inside the gate. The house was made of dull red brick. The roof seemed too small for it, and the windows, which were always closed, were set at the corners. There was a washline in the yard and a pen for the turkeys. Oom Poen's old turquoise Chev had been left up on blocks with the bonnet open.

On the way back from Kareebos Rosie's father stopped in the dusty yard near the siding and said, 'I just want to tell Oom Poen that I'd like the truck to collect my mohair this week, Rosie. I won't be long.' And he went across to the little tin office by the tracks and disappeared inside.

It was very hot waiting in the yard and Rosie glanced down at the sack at her feet. She could see that the hare was panting with small, shallow breaths. She looked over at the reservoir beside the fence of Jacoba Pandoer's garden and she opened the door of the truck and got out.

She lifted the sack and loosened its mouth. She went across the stony ground and dipped her fingers into the warm, oily water of the tank. Then she slipped her hand in towards the hare's head, coaxing it to drink. She tried again and again, speaking reassuring words.

Jacoba Pandoer had been feeding her turkeys when the truck arrived. She walked across the grass to the fence and watched Rosie dabbling her hand in the water and talking to herself. She said nothing, only watched. Rosie glanced up and was still. Jacoba Pandoer stared back.

Jacoba Pandoer was not an old woman – but at the same time she seemed to be a woman who had never been young. She was big, with the arms of a man. She could have lifted sacks or bales with the roadworkers and tossed them into the back of the trailer hitched to the big cream and maroon bus if she had wanted.

Her eyes were wayward. Rather like the windows of her house, she gazed from the corners. Rosie was not

sure how to look at her directly. She came towards Rosie, almost shuffling, for the sides of her shoes had been split to give more spread to her feet.

'What animal have you got in that sack?' said Jacoba Pandoer. Her voice was low and gruff – quite unexpected in its softness.

Rosie held the sack tightly. 'How do you know I've got an animal in here?' she said.

'By the way you hold your arms, like you scared of being bitten.'

Rosie backed a little. She did not want Jacoba Pandoer to touch the hare with her big hands. But Jacoba Pandoer came through the gate and stood quite close, with her grey jersey buttoned up in the wrong holes and her downcast eyes peering sideways from their corners. 'What is it?' she said again.

'I got it on Kareebos,' replied Rosie warily. 'The jackal-catcher must have caught it. It was tied up. My Dad says he was probably going to eat it.'

Jacoba Pandoer took the sack and folded it back. The hare lay limp. Jacoba cocked her head and peered at it and then she said, 'Do you know this animal?'

'Of course,' said Rosie, a little importantly because she was familiar with all the animals of the veld. 'It's a scrub hare.'

'No,' said Jacoba Pandoer. 'It's a *doekvoetjie*.' She closed the sack gently.

'A *doekvoetjie*?' said Rosie.

'I haven't seen one for donkey's years,' said Jacoba in her small, gruff way. 'You don't find them in the veld any more. We used to have them on my Oupa's place

23

near Deelfontein. They run slow. They shake their feet.' She gestured with her hands. 'You can catch them with a dog.' She touched the sack. 'There was this old *Boesman*,' she looked away and paused. 'He told me it was used for *muti* to call jackals and *rooikatte*. The old *Boesman* said it was once a child that the moon made into a hare. Now things die because of it.' Rosie glanced at her uncomfortably. 'It's strong *muti* for the old *Boesmans*, this hare,' said Jacoba Pandoer.

Rosie's father was coming back across the yard from the office. Oom Poen was standing by the door saying goodbye and pulling at his braces with his thumbs. Rosie said, 'I better go.'

'What you going to do with the *doekvoet*?' asked Jacoba.

'I'll put it with my white rabbits.'

'You will never make it tame,' said Jacoba Pandoer, more to herself than to Rosie. 'It is a wild thing.'

3

When she got home Rosie moved the lamb into another pen and put the sack in that hutch, next to the white rabbits. She made a bed of straw and fetched a bowl of food and then took the hare from the sack and laid it down. The little animal crept like a wounded thing into a corner. The white rabbits sniffed at it through the wire netting. They bobbed and hopped on soft white feet, pink eyes curious. The hare did not move. It hardly seemed to breathe.

A while later Skip came home, bringing Willie Tromp with him. They flung their bicycles against the hedge and crowded round.

'Where'd you get that *kolhaas*?' said Willie Tromp, poking a finger at it through the wire.

'It's not a *kolhaas*,' said Rosie, 'and it's very frightened, so please don't bother it.'

'It's a funny-looking hare,' said Skip.

'It's a *doekvoet*,' said Rosie. 'They say it's rare.'

'*Ag*, man,' said Willie.' 'You can see it's just a *kolhaas*.'

'Doesn't look like one to me,' said Skip, who knew the animals on the farm even better than Rosie.

'It's a *doekvoet*,' said Rosie.

'Who told you?' asked Skip.

'Jacoba Pandoer,' replied Rosie, without thinking.

'Jacoba Pandoer?'

'Yes.'

'Did you talk to Jacoba Pandoer?'

'Yes.'

'But she's mad,' interrupted Willie. 'Everyone knows she done something dreadful once.'

'What?'

'She ran away from the Welfare Home at De Aar.'

'So?'

'My Pa says what can you expect when someone only wants to live in the *strooise* and talk to people walking in the road. My Pa says that's why she is mad.'

'Why?'

'Because who'd want to live with *Boesmans* in a *strooihuis*? Tell me that!'

'Maybe she likes them!'

'Well, she run away from De Aar into the bush. Only mad people do that, Rosie. My Pa says . . .'

'I don't care what your Pa says,' retorted Rosie.

'You'll go mad like Jacoba Pandoer, Rosie. My Pa

says there's a lot of mad people in that family because of her, so you better watch out.'

'Rosie!' interrupted Skip. 'You still haven't said what kind of hare it is.'

'Dad looked it up and he thinks that it's a Bushman hare,' said Rosie. 'There's another name for it as well. A *pondhaas* or something like that.'

'What's that mean?'

'Long ago there was a scientist who said he'd pay a pound to anyone who brought him one.'

'What's a pound?' asked Willie.

'An old kind of money they used to have.'

'Maybe you should sell this hare to him and get some money to buy more rabbits,' suggested Willie Tromp. 'They look nice with their pink eyes.'

'Don't be silly,' said Rosie. 'The scientist died ages ago.' She glanced at her rabbits, feeling suddenly scornful of their pale fur and their eyes like toy rubies.

'If you don't like these rabbits any more I'll have them,' said Willie. 'Anyway, they better than this old *kolhaas*.'

'It's not a *kolhaas*,' said Skip impatiently. 'I've never seen one like it before.'

'There are hardly any left.' Rosie felt important then. 'Anyway, it's really a riverine rabbit and it's endangered so I have to look after it properly and tame it and make sure it doesn't die, because Dad says scientists are very interested in it.'

Skip looked grave and Willie stared at her as though he didn't understand at all. Rosie turned to the hare, wishing suddenly that she had never gone into the

28

shed at Kareebos and pried among the trapper's secrets. For here was the little hare – the *doekvoet* or the
river rabbit or the *pondhaas* or whatever it was called –
dying slowly in the pen.

She didn't know whether to be angry with the trapper for catching it for *muti* or angry with her father for
wanting his jackals hunted or angry with herself for
interfering. So she turned on Willie Tromp and got
angry with him instead and she said, 'How'd you like
someone to be always poking their fingers into your
ears or eyes, Willie Tromp? Leave the hare alone!' And
even Willie looked surprised for he had been sitting
very still with his hands on his knees, listening.

'What's its name?' asked Skip.

'It hasn't got one yet.'

'Lets call it Hansie,' said Skip, who liked allitera-
tions. 'Hansie Hare.'

'It's supposed to be a rabbit!' said Rosie, sensing that
the little creature lying in the straw was far too wild to
have a name as tame as that.

Evening came and a cold, small wind blew in from the
hills. Still the little hare had not touched its food.
Rosie's mother suggested warm milk and porridge.
Her father shook his head and told her to turn it free.
Dan tried to stroke its nose but it shrank away. Rosie
sat with it, not knowing what to do. She had always
been able to coax life out of small creatures, patient to
the end. But this was different. It seemed as though the
hare did not want to live.

Restlessly she wandered into the house but she was

unable to play with Dan or talk to Skip the way she always had. She hardly ate her supper for she knew that out there in the yard the hare lay, nose against the wire, waiting to die. She went to bed and fell asleep. She dreamed that the hare had grown huge and that it followed her, jackal tail wound around its head, and that Jacoba Pandoer was digging turnips from the ground.

She awoke and lay staring at the dark shape of the cypress tree against the sky. She wondered if she shouldn't creep outside and open the door of the hutch so that the *pondhaas* could escape. But then she knew that if it did, it would be far, far from the place where the trapper had found it. Maybe it would never find its home again.

She wondered if perhaps she ought to take it to the trapper and give it back to him. But then she thought of how she'd found it tethered to the food-trough, a sacrifice for jackals.

If it was going to die it might be better, after all, if she killed it by herself – quickly, painlessly – with Skip's little hatchet. She had watched the stockmen slaughter goats, pigs and sheep since she was small. It had never worried her before. But to take the hare, to hold it and to cut its throat would be quite different. Like the goat that had lost its horn, the blood would drip down over her hands all hot and thick and red . . .

If she was not brave enough either to kill it or to let it free, she would have to find a way to make it eat. But she did not know what herbs or plants or grasses it might choose. Only Tantyi Mayekiso knew those things and she dared not go to him. For maybe – just maybe – Willie Tromp was right for once. Maybe the trapper did become a jackal in the dark.

Rosie kicked her blankets off and turned her pillow to make it cool. There was no one who could help her. No one. Except, perhaps, Jacoba Pandoer.

In the morning, just as it was getting light, Rosie got up and crept outside. Only her father was about. She could hear the sound of his boots as he walked across the kitchen yard towards the dairy. She climbed out of her window and went to the rabbit hutches. The hare had not moved. Still it breathed, still it laid its ears quite flat along its back. The pink-eyed rabbits huddled in their nest and the little orphan lamb watched her from its bed of straw.

Rosie took her bicycle from the shed and rode away down the road as fast as she could. A blue crane drifted among the bushes trailing tail-feathers grey as wood-smoke, and she heard a korhaan near the furrow.

She passed the gate where the letter-box was nailed to a pole and a herd of goats browsed, looking small and white, like a flock of egrets roosting in a bush. She passed the store and reached the siding where the roadworkers' houses stood together on their dusty plots of grass.

She leant her bike against the fence and opened the Pandoers' gate. It squeaked a warning. The sunflower hung its heavy head above the path and Rosie could see where birds had picked out its big black seeds. She tiptoed up the polished steps to the back door. Her heart beat painfully inside her chest but she knocked: a hollow, timid little knock because she was afraid.

She waited, remembering how Willie had said Jacoba Pandoer was mad and that she'd done something dreadful. Maybe she had murdered someone. Maybe she would lock Rosie in the coalshed and come and stare at her sometimes with her wayward eyes while she decided what to do with her. All Rosie would be able to see through the cracks in the shutter would be the sunflower with its drooping head, dropping its seeds onto the ground as if they were rotten teeth.

She could hear Jacoba Pandoer. She could hear her step – the scuff of her shoes, the dark shadow suddenly at the gap beneath the door. Rosie backed into the sunlight so she could run.

'*Ja*?' said Jacoba Pandoer without surprise, as she stood looking down at Rosie. She wore the same old grey jersey over her dress, the same old shoes. Rosie turned her head sideways, just a little – without meaning to – so she could look at Jacoba Pandoer with one eye, the way Jacoba looked at her.

'Do you remember the *doekvoet*?' said Rosie.

'*Ja*.'

'It's still alive but I'm scared it might die. I don't know what to do.'

For a moment Jacoba said nothing and Rosie shuffled her feet and glanced into the kitchen beyond. Last year's calender from the butcher-shop hung on a nail high up on the wall and an enamel teapot and plate of bread stood on the table where Jacoba had been eating her breakfast.

Jacoba unfolded her arms. 'Let it free,' she said.

'The dogs would get it,' said Rosie. 'I want to keep it but I don't know what it eats.'

'Ask the *Boesman* you got it from.'

Rosie stared at her. 'Willie Tromp says . . .'

But Jacoba Pandoer did not seem to know Willie Tromp and she said, 'You can never make it tame, *meisie*. The old *Boesmans* – even they know that.'

'I'm too scared to speak to him . . .'

'Why?' said Jacoba Pandoer, as if it never occured to her to be afraid of someone like Tantyi Mayekiso. And the way she looked at Rosie then was as though – suddenly – she, Rosie, was the stranger.

Rosie said, very meekly, 'Where do you think I'll find him?'

Jacoba turned her head towards the ridge where the great cleft rock rose up. The kannabos that grew between the halves was feathery and faint against the sky as a bird's print is upon the ground.

'I'll go then,' said Rosie, backing away. 'I'll ask him.'

'You should set it free. Even if it dies. It is better than a cage,' said Jacoba Pandoer. 'This thing I know.' And then she closed the door and left Rosie suddenly alone, standing in the dusty path.

As Rosie turned away and started towards the gate, Willie Tromp's father passed in his truck with Willie sitting in the front beside him. He gaped at Rosie. She felt like sticking out her tongue at him but instead she pretended that she had not seen him and she took her bicycle, mounted it and rode away towards the turning to Kareebos. She crossed the grid and stopped to look around. She was alone. All alone. On Kareebos there was no one. Only Tantyi Mayekiso, the jackal-trapper.

4

It was still, already hot. There were four gates to open.
Rosie bumped along the uneven track, glancing from
side to side. The bushes seemed to cluster around her,
watching. She reached the first gate, the second, the
third. Near the fourth grew a boerboon tree and its
scaly grey shade spread out across the sand. Rosie
opened the gate, which swung back, thudded against
the trunk. Something fell and rolled across her foot.
She cried out and jumped away. A stone, smooth and
water-weathered, lay in the dust. It had fallen from a
place where a branch had been cut. The heartwood was
delicate and pale. She looked at it, surprised: there was
something tender deep within the craggy boerboon
after all.

She picked up the stone and placed it back where it

had lain. She knew it had been put there as an offering to the spirit of the tree, just as travellers place stones on cairns and say, '*Qamata, ndiphe amandla*' – 'God, give strength to me': a blessing for the journey.

She closed the gate again and took the path that led down to the shed. She went inside but it was empty. Even the skins of the jackal and the *rooikat* had gone. She left her bicycle leaning up against the watertank. Then she climbed the fence and started out across the veld.

It lay still and cool and blue before her, stretching out towards the ridge. On the crest she could see the great cleft rock from which, some people said, the old diviner fell so long ago. The kloof below was a place where no one went – not stockmen, goats, sheep or cows. It was trackless but for trails made by wild things. Unexplored except when horses passed and buck and jackals crept away until the silence had returned. No one had ventured there in years, except the trapper, Tantyi Mayekiso. He knew each path, each tree, and how the wind – from east or west – might catch the leaves.

And on that day he sat against a fallen trunk where lichen grew and watched as Rosie walked across the veld towards the kloof. Small as a hare herself, jinking almost – here, there – in between the bushes. He waited, sensing why it was that she had come.

When Rosie reached the edge of the trees she stopped. Then, drawing in her breath, she called the trapper's name: 'Tantyi Mayekiso!' The trapper turned his head. He did not need to speak, for the movement in all the stillness made her look.

Rosie stood, transfixed. She could feel the strange, strong beat of her heart urging her to run away. But she stayed quite still, and said in Xhosa in a voice both small and hoarse, 'I have come because of the hare that I took from you.'

She approached cautiously. The light between the leaves was like the still reflections in a water-hole and Rosie watched the shadows tremble on the rocks around her.

The trapper said, 'It is Dhau?'

'Dhau?'

'Dhau,' replied the trapper. 'The hare. That is he.'

'I wished to keep him,' said Rosie. 'I did not want you to kill him.' The trapper looked at her in silence and Rosie hurried on, almost in a whisper. 'He will not eat,' she said. 'Do you know perhaps what food he likes?'

'He will not eat because his spirit is angry towards you.'

'I do not want to hurt him! I only want to make him tame. Why should he be angry?'

'Dhau is the child of the old people,' replied Tantyi Mayekiso. 'It was Dhau that was there when the world began and the moon was very new.' He raised his hand and drew the moon, sickle-thin.

'It is Dhau that drinks the water of the moon and brings the words of life and death. This is his work. It is Dhau that was once a child that the moon has made into a hare. That is why Dhau is slow-footed like a man, timid as a child. It is still the man in Dhau the jackal smells and that is why he comes to find him – for is not a man a hunter? And is not a jackal that which follows where a hunter goes?'

The trapper turned his eyes to her and spoke to her directly. 'This I know,' he said. 'It is my work to know the ways of Jackal and of Dhau.' He paused. 'Here,' he said, 'you will find *Mvundla*, who is busy with the things of hares. But Dhau – he is the child of the old people and like them he is almost gone.'

'If he is nearly gone,' said Rosie, 'why do you catch him to make *mutis* for trapping jackals?'

'It is my work. I too have children who wait for food.' The trapper stopped. Rosie did not speak. She looked up towards the rock high above her. The branches of the kannabos spiralled out and up as though once – as a seedling – it had thrust its way, piece by piece until it split the rock so it could touch the sky.

Rosie turned back to him and said, 'I do not know what food it likes.'

'It will not want to live if the *isithunzi* that it has is gone.'

'What is *isithunzi*?' said Rosie.

'His shadow,' said the trapper as though that were enough for her to understand.

Rosie looked down at her own shadow crouched beside her. 'Why should its shadow die?' she said doubtfully.

'You cannot keep Dhau with a sheep,' said the trapper, as though he had crept up to the pen at night to see what she had done with it. 'What are sheep but ticks on the hide of the earth, without *isithunzi*, or wisdom.

38

Rosie thought of her father's stock moving across the camps, pale-eyed and foolish. 'What must I do?'

'When it has died you can eat it,' he said, as if there was no other choice.

'If I feed it, it will live.'

'Dhau is dead like a goat but walking still upon its legs.' The trapper raised his hand to his chin in dismissal. 'The meat is good. And even yet the jackal speaks of this.'

'You just want it back for *muti*!' said Rosie defensively.

'What use is it to me now that it has lost its *isithunzi*?' said the trapper. 'Without that, it is nothing.'

'Is there any way to get its *isithunzi* back?'

'When the moon is small and Dhau can grow with it in brightness – only then can its spirit be restored.'

'I do not understand.'

'Have you never seen the shadow that is Dhau's up there inside the moon when it is bright and full? Have you never watched him grow? Here then are his ears. Here his head. Here his back. Here then are the feet of Dhau. His *isithunzi* grows and then it dies and grows again as does the moon's.'

Rosie thought of this, remembering how her Grandmother had always said there was a man's face in the moon and how she'd doubted it ever since the night when Skip had cried impatiently, 'It's not a man, Grandma! It's a hare!' Everyone had laughed and Skip had said quite crossly, 'Nomatse told me that and I can see it! So!'

'I will bring you to the plants that Dhau must eat,'

Tantyi Mayekiso said. 'Put him in a place where it is dark and feed him, for he does not like the day and wants to be alone. But if you wish to have his *isithunzi* grow you must let him free and give him to the moon when it is small.'

Rosie nodded, saying nothing. She did not fully understand his words. She hoped that if the hare began to eat she'd find a way to tame him slowly, so he wouldn't be afraid or angry.

Tantyi Mayekiso stood and beckoned to her. He made no sound as he started down the hill. Walking in his shabby clothes with his loose, swinging step he seemed no different from a stockman or a herder. Rosie followed, knowing that she'd never thought a man like Tantyi Mayekiso might exist – a man who kept secrets of the jackals and who knew the story of the little hare called Dhau. She wondered why it was that only Tant Jacoba seemed to understand these things and why it was that people called her mad.

They went into a culvert where once a stream had flowed and Tantyi Mayekiso bent beside a clump of plants and broke off little branches.

'Where did you find Dhau?' asked Rosie as she stood and watched.

'In the night. Where the shadow of the rock lies down.'

He pointed and Rosie followed his gaze across the veld to where the morning shadow of the great diviner's rock lay dark upon the ground.

She took the plants from him and looked at them, knowing both their feel and smell. They had always seemed so small and ordinary before, growing as they did along the irrigation furrows or beside the stream. She had never thought to ask their name. But now she carried them with care so that no leaf might drop, no twiglet fall. She went as though she'd just received the secrets of the moon and held them in her arms.

She took her bike and rode away. She passed the first gate by the boerboon tree. Still the little pebble lay balanced where the branch was cut. She passed the second and the third and when she reached the district road the sun was high and hot and all the shadows of the bush had shrunk and gone.

She freewheeled down the hill and passed the empty shed and the siding and the roadworkers' houses. Jacoba Pandoer was standing at her door and Rosie slowed a little, waved, half-pointing at the plants tied to her handlebars. But Jacoba Pandoer just stood, leaning up against the doorframe. She simply watched in quietness until Rosie and the bicycle had disappeared.

5

Rosie took the hare from the hutch between the rabbits and the lamb. She carried it to a small tackroom behind the workshop, where no one ever went. She made a nest and lined it with the plants she had brought from Kareebos. The hare seemed weak and yet its fierceness had not gone. Almost it bared its teeth at her as she set it down. She closed the door and went away.

A little later Skip came hurrying over from the pens to find her. 'Rosie! Hansie isn't in the *hok*! He's gone!' he cried, shaking his head so his hair stuck up as though it was anguished too. 'I've looked every-where,' he said. 'I even crawled through the pipe across the *sloot* to see if he was hiding. One of the dogs might get him. I bet Dan let him out. I saw him hanging around the *hok* this morning. I'll clout him if I catch him!'

'It wasn't Dan,' said Rosie. 'I put the hare in the tackroom. The trapper said he needs to be alone so don't tell Dan or Willie.'

'The trapper?' Skip was astonished.

Rosie nodded.

'When did you speak to him?' he almost whispered.

Rosie led him to the tackroom where she had hidden the hare and then she told him all the trapper had said. 'Promise you won't tell,' she finished. 'Promise!'

Skip licked his finger and held it up and said, 'Strike me dead if I do! And when Willie came later in the day and said, 'Where's the *kolhaas*?' Skip replied, 'Don'no. We think Dan let him out.'

'Didn't!' protested Dan, who had followed Willie. He began to wail while his small friends gazed on solemnly.

'Never mind, Dan,' said Rosie. 'Maybe he didn't like it in the *hok* and wanted to get out.'

Willie looked at her puzzled. 'Why aren't you upset, Rosie?' he said. 'It's you who always cries when something dies and we have to have a funeral.'

It was true. There were graves below the hedge all marked out with stones where they had buried lambs, birds, mice, and once a small rhebok.

'You should have tied him up till he was tame,' said Willie. 'My Pa had to tie Adoonsie, our baboon. If Hansie had been tied he wouldn't have got away. My Pa made lots of meercats tame when he was small.'

Maybe we'll still find him,' said Rosie hurriedly. 'Let's go and look,' and she turned away, leading them from the shed.

Some hours later Rosie crept barefooted to the window of the tackroom. She rubbed clean a small place on the dusty pane and looked in. At first she could see nothing and then, when her eyes had become accustomed to the gloom, she saw that Dhau had moved. He sat crouched, not flattened – his eyes open. She could see the delicate veining of an ear as he turned his head towards the light.

Rosie smiled to herself. 'Dhau,' she said softly, thinking of how they'd named him Hansie and how it would seem as strange to call him Hansie now as it would to think of Tantyi Mayekiso as Klaas or Jacob or Witbooi.

The little hare went back to its nest and crouched as though it meant to sleep. Rosie could barely see it in the shadow of the straw. It seemed so solitary, so alone. She watched, rapt, like a mother standing by a sleeping child, warm with pride for having made it but – having done that – full of fear for all its life.

Rosie turned from the window and looked up. Willie Tromp was watching her. Half hidden behind the stiff, straight leaves of a *garingboom* he stood and gazed at her with a strange, anxious expression on his face.

For a moment Rosie hestitated, not knowing what to do. Then she bent slowly, picked up some stones that had fallen from the wall and piled them carefully one on top of the other on the ground. She rocked back and forth, mumbling to herself, just loud enough for Willie Tromp to hear. *'Qamata, ndiphe amandla,'* she said. She walked around the offering as an old Xhosa woman might, passing a cairn on a journey.

45

'What you doing?' said Willie Tromp, coming forward a little cautiously.

'I'm asking the ancestors to bring Hansie back,' she said, as though it was the most natural thing in the world for her to speak to them.

Willie gazed at her and swallowed. 'You mad, Rosie! I said to Skip, ever since you spoke to Tannie Pandoer and she told you about what was Hansie, you mad!'

Rosie gave Willie Tromp a mysterious look. She tried to make her eyes peer out sideways like Tant Jacoba's and Willie said accusingly, 'My Pa says she used to talk to herself when she was small, just like you. My Pa says she was always muttering in Xhosa like she was crazy. You see – you just the same.'

Rosie tossed her head and walked deliberately past him.

'Jacoba Pandoer! Jacoba Pandoer!' he taunted. He ran after her, nudging at her with his elbow. 'They'll take you away and lock you up like they took her once!'

Rosie turned on him and shouted, 'Leave me, Willie Tromp!' and she could feel the tears coming suddenly, when she had believed that he could never make her cry.

She ran across the yard, Willie in pursuit. He grabbed at her but Rosie shook him off and Oukan, who was digging in the bed below the kitchen window, looked up in surprise as Willie leapt across at Rosie, scattering earth and stones with his clumsy feet. Oukan grunted and shook his trowel at Willie, chasing him off.

Rosie dodged through the kitchen and stopped in

the passage to rub her fists angrily into her eyes. But it did not help – the tears would not go away.

It seemed as though a terrible truth had been shown to her. Willie had said she was like Jacoba Pandoer. What if he was right? 'My Pa says . . .': fathers always told the truth. At least, hers did. Why not Willie's?

Rosie went to find her mother in the garden. She wanted to stand close to her and feel her there and ask if it were possible that she might grow up like Jacoba. But then she stopped, knowing that she couldn't tell her mother anything without explaining to her why Willie Tromp had called her that and why it was that Hansie was a hare called Dhau. She did not think her mother would believe in *isithunzi* – and anyway, she wasn't sure she knew what *isithunzi* was except that somehow it seemed to be important to the trapper and he didn't want the hare without it.

Rosie stamped up the verandah steps and banged the front door behind her. Hearing the thud echo through the house made her feel better so she slammed her bedroom door as well. Who cared about what Willie Tromp and his Pa had said? Everyone knew Willie's father was as thick as a goat – just like Willie! They were both the same! So there!

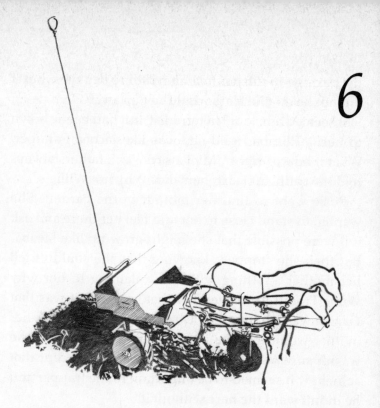

6

It was Auntie Dorcas's birthday and everyone had
been invited for lunch. Grandma had made a special
cake and as soon as it was iced they all set out in the big
car with Rosie and Skip in the back and Dan – all
scrubbed and washed for once – sitting on Grandma's
knee. Even Skip had been persuaded to put on shoes –
something he never did at home. Their father wore a
tie and jacket and had wetted his hair so it lay flat and
neat, although it seemed to Rosie that it might spring
up at any moment, all unruly like her own.

Their mother played 'I-spy' with them because it was
the only way to keep Dan's mind off feeling car-sick
and from arguing about the gates that he was still too
small to open.

The dust spiralled out behind the car and the wheels rattled on the cattle-grids. They passed Oom Poen Pandoer standing by his grader. He raised his hat in greeting. Rosie turned and looked to see if Tant Jacoba was anywhere about but the yard was empty. She kept on looking till the house was small and brown and far, the sunflower like a little yellow flag beside the gate.

Skip nudged her, showing where he'd scooped a fingerful of icing from the cake he was holding on his lap. Rosie glanced at Grandma to see if she had noticed and then she took a secret lick herself. Maybe just today Auntie Dorcas would forget about the fish-paste sandwiches and give them chocolate cake instead.

It was hot. Willie Tromp was bored. His parents were asleep in their room. They always rested on Saturday afternoons and he was not allowed to make a noise. His sisters were playing somewhere in an irrigation furrow with the farm children and he did not want to join them. He decided to go to Skip's. They could build more roads for their wire-cars on the slopes behind the workshop. Maybe they could catch some of the mice living in the creeper by the kitchen door and tie them in as drivers. Trapping fieldmice was one of Willie's favourite games. He took his wire-car and set off down the road.

The yard at Skip's was empty. An old tortoise, neck outstretched, peered at Willie as he passed the vegetable garden. Willie went up the steps and knocked at the back door but no one came. He clanged on the iron pipe hanging in the thorn tree by the gate. Oukan –

rather tortoise-like himself – was pottering among the flowerbeds. He saw Willie and, grunting, waved his arms at him to go away – no one was allowed to strike the gong on Saturdays.

Willie ran off and hid in the shed. He peeped through the window to see if Oukan was following. After a while he slipped out and went around the back to see if there were any goat kids in the pen. He pushed his wire-car along the kraal wall and then he raced it right across the open stretch of ground towards the tackroom.

He glanced through the window and he stopped. He pressed his nose against the glass. He stared. On the floor, half hidden in the straw, he saw the hare. He wiped the place where his breath had misted up the pane and looked again. He opened the door and crept inside.

The hare started from its sleep and Willie stood quite still. He wondered how it had got there. Someone, he was sure, had found it and hidden it from Rosie and from Skip. Perhaps that someone wished to eat it. Willie thought about this as he squatted on the ground. If he took it now, he'd save it and Skip and even Rosie would be pleased. Perhaps they'd let him keep it in the term when they were far away at school. He would make a *hok* and show Rosie he could tame it just as well as she.

But then, Willie thought, when they came home again they'd want it back. Willie looked down at the hare and knew he couldn't let them take it once he'd fed and cared for it and anyway, there were five white

rabbits in the hutch which was enough for anyone to manage.

Rosie, Willie decided, had neglected them since the day she'd found the hare. He'd be doing the rabbits a favour if he took it. Rosie too. Perhaps she was relieved it had escaped. It seemed as though she might be. She was even acting like herself since Hansie'd gone. He could see why someone might prefer the rabbits. He did. Hansie was brown and fierce and thin with a funny black line along his jaw but the rabbits were big and soft with their glassy, ruby eyes. Still, Willie thought, Hansie was better than nothing.

Willie found an empty grain-bag. He crept towards the hare, then suddenly lunged and grabbed it by the leg. He hoisted it up, dropped it into the sack and tied the opening.

He went outside triumphantly and picked up his wire-car. He hurried away across the yard, bumping into Oukan at the corner of the kraal. Oukan stared at Willie accusingly.

'It's just an old sack,' said Willie, turning away.

Oukan grasped Willie's arm and shook it.

'It's none of your business, you silly old *mompara*!' exclaimed Willie rudely. He wriggled out of Oukan's grip, sidestepped and dodged away.

Oukan shook his fist. He did not like other people hanging around when the family was out. He went back to the garden muttering to himself as Willie hurried up the road towards his own farm gate.

Willie peeped into the sack and grinned to himself. He had found Hansie! Locked up, too! It must have

been Oukan who had put him in the shed to hide him. It was just like the old *skelm* to do a thing like that, Willie thought. And Oukan, Willie knew, would never tell on him because – he laughed – what could Oukan say when he couldn't even speak? Willie felt rather pleased with himself for rescuing Hansie from the pot.

He put the hare in the coalshed with some water and a pile of carrot-tops and cabbage leaves and went to find a box and wire to build a hutch. He would make him tame just as his father had made Adoonsie tame.

Adoonsie was a young baboon his Pa had once found in the veld when he'd been hunting. He had tied him to a post where he could climb and play beside the guava tree. Adoonsie liked to throw down guavas. He could make you roll with laughter – like the time he got fat Ekkies in the eye and there were pips stuck in his beard and he had been so cross.

But the best had been the day he'd tricked Adoonsie and left a rubber snake by the water-dish. Adoonsie had screamed and screamed and sat shivering at the top of the pole until Willie's mother had taken the snake away.

Willie found an old tea-chest and some chicken-wire and lifted down his father's pliers from the workshop wall. He carried them all to the coalshed and sat in the sun outside the the door.

In the afternoon – just before the time the birds are busy in the coolness and the coot and the yellowbills slide out across the dams – Tantyi Mayekiso gathered up his things and slung his bag on his back and set out from Kareebos. He came across the hills, along the ridge and down through the stock-camps to the homestead, bringing with him all the jackal skins and *rooikat* pelts. He stood in the yard and waited. When Oukan looked up from the flowerbeds and saw him he came over hesitantly, keeping his distance, for there was no one else about to see the trapper standing by the back door. Oukan hurried away to fetch the senior stockman, who had been left the money for his pay.

Tantyi Mayekiso laid the skins near the water-tank and glanced around. He saw the orphan lamb and the five white rabbits in their hutches. He smelled their bland, tame smell. He saw no sign that Dhau had been there once. He turned away and when the stockman came he took his money, touched his hand to his jackal-tail hat and saying nothing further than a greeting slipped away like a shadow through the yard.

He took again the path across the stony hills and uplands, where grass birds call sorrowfully in the wind. He left no footprints where he walked. He disappeared as though he had never come at all.

7

When Rosie returned home from Auntie Dorcas's she threw off her dress and dragged on her jeans and T-shirt. She went to feed the rabbits and the lamb and then she ran across the yard and down towards the furrow to pick some fresh green twigs for the hare. Skip was wheeling his bicycle out of the shed.

'Where're you off to?' asked Rosie.

'Ma said Willie could come and spend the night because we are going back to school next week and anyway she and Dad are invited to a party or something in town this evening so we can have a midnight feast if you like. Only don't say anything to Dan because he'll tell Nomatse and then she'll call Gran and that will spoil it.' Skip mounted his bike, circled and raced along the track towards the cattle-grid. He flew across it with a practised swoop so that the irons rang.

When Rosie had picked all she wanted in the furrow she went to the dairy for a bowl of water and carried it round to the tackroom. She was so startled to see the door hanging on its old hinges and letting in the brightness of the afternoon that she dropped the dish and the water slopped across her dusty feet.

She ran inside and searched around but the hare had gone. 'Dhau!' she cried. 'Dhau! Where are you?' She examined the ground, looking for tracks – a jackal, a *rooikat*, a dog – but all she could find were dozens of different human prints and the two bumpy lines where a wire-car had been pushed across the sand.

She hurried to the hutches, hoping that Oukan or perhaps Nomatse had discovered the hare and had put it in the pen but it was empty. Rosie turned, looking for someone – anyone – who could tell her where the hare might be. By the kitchen door, lying below the watertank – copper, ears tufted black – she saw the *rooikat* pelts, and beside them the jackal skins.

Rosie stooped to them and touched them, knowing Tantyi Mayekiso had been there. He'd come when no one was at home – silently, in the quiet of the afternoon – and found the hare. He'd taken it, she knew.

She ran to the workshop and pulled her bicycle outside. She bumped off along the track, the wind flying in her face. When she reached the district road she peddled up the slope to a place where she could see the road curving down towards the trading-store. It was empty. There was no one. Rosie stood, listening to the wind. It seemed lonely and discontented – as though it came from far-off stony places, without the taste of summer rain. She turned her bicycle and mounted slowly, riding back towards the farm. Tantyi Mayekiso had come, when no one had been there to challenge him. He'd taken back the hare from her, believing it was his and now he'd kill it and make it into *muti*. He'd tricked her with his stories of its *isithunzi*! There was no such thing!

As Rosie passed the dam she met Skip and Willie Tromp racing each other on their bicycles. Willie's old green pyjamas were wrapped around his handle-bars. The legs billowed out beside him, dipping and shaking as he hit the sandy bumps in the track.

'Guess what?' said Skip, turning and riding along-side Rosie. 'Willie's Pa said he could have some white rabbits.'

'How come he changed his mind?' said Rosie.

'Don'no,' mumbled Willie, not looking at her.

'That *hok* you were making looked a bit small to me,' said Skip.

'*Ag*, man,' said Willie, 'that's only for the meantime.'

'If you use it you must have a run in the front so the rabbits can eat in the grass. You'll have to sink some wire so they can't dig their way out.

'*Ja*,' said Willie, 'I'll do it when I get them,' and he suddenly peddled ahead, zigzagging across the road, back and forth. The sun seemed to shine hotly on his ears, making them red and flushed.

Rosie glanced at him. She was about to call after him but she changed her mind and dropped back a little and when the boys had gone into the house she went to find Oukan.

He was standing by the kraal-wall smoking his pipe, the sheepdog sitting at his feet.

'Oukan,' said Rosie, looking into his face so that he could see her mouth, 'did you see a hare?' She made a hopping motion. 'The one, Oukan, that used to be in the *hok*. You know him?' Oukan frowned and took his pipe slowly from his mouth.

'The trapper was here, Oukan. Tantyi Mayekiso.' Oukan looked intently at her.

'Tan-tyi Ma-ye-ki-so,' she repeated and put her hand to her head and fluttered her fingers as if she was touching her jackal-tail hat. 'The tackroom, Oukan,' she pointed towards the door. 'Did he go in there?'

Oukan grunted and pointed to his palm as though he were receiving something. Then he shook his head and gestured towards the tackroom. He grunted again, tilted his hat, cupped his fingers behind his ears and pointed down the road, moving his hands as though he were pushing a wire-car.

'The one with ears like this?' said Rosie, mimicking. Oukan grinned.

'Willie Tromp!' she said. 'I might have guessed!'

Rosie went past the hutches and peeped through the kitchen door. Her mother was pouring orange juice for Willie and Skip. Dan was foraging in the biscuit tin. Rosie slipped away to fetch her bicycle again. She wheeled it across the yard and lifted it over the grid so no one would hear her. Then she started out for Willie's house.

When she reached the Tromps' farm-gate she left her

bicycle behind a bush and walked up the drive in the shadow of the quince hedge, keeping her head low. She did not wish to meet anyone: not Mr Tromp nor old Ekkies the gardener, not Baas the bull-terrier, nor Willie's little sisters. She looked over at the house. The windows were closed. The flyscreen was fastened across the front door. Mrs Tromp's baskets of ferns hung together in the shadow of the stoep.

Rosie went to the shearing-shed, the workshop, the feed-room, wondering where Willie had put the hare. Behind the garages she found the packing-case which he had been making into a hutch. It was pushed against the wall of the coalshed, and the pliers and chicken-wire and nails were lying scattered around as though he'd left them in a hurry.

It was very quiet. The windmill turned slowly by the reservoir, its long shadow flickering round. But closer than the sound of the windmill, closer and quieter and more secret, Rosie could hear a soft scratching. So soft, so small was it, it was like a dry leaf turning across the ground.

It seemed to be coming from the coalshed. Rosie crept towards the door. Then she turned, startled – almost crying out – for Willie's father strode round the corner, pipe clenched between his teeth. 'Rosie!' he exclaimed, as startled as she.

Rosie backed against the door. 'Hello, Oom Dolf,' she said. She could feel that her neck and face and ears were burning. 'I came,' she said, 'to find my brother Skip.'

'No, Rosie, he and Willie, they went to your place

some time ago.'

'I didn't see them,' said Rosie. 'Well,' she continued hurriedly, looking up at him and trying to keep the tremble from her voice, 'Skip told me you're going to let Willie have rabbits.' The blood was thumping in her ears as she spoke. 'Look, he's been making a *hok*.'

'Rabbits, *se voet*!' muttered Mr Tromp. 'If Willie must keep pets then there are enough *hanslammetjies* and *tollies* on this farm to make him happy. There is no profit in a rabbit! My own father used to say, "Dolf, my boy – if there's no profit then there's no point" – that's what he used to say!'

'Anyway,' Rosie twisted her fingers into her ponytail and shifted from one foot to the other. 'I better go home before it gets dark, I suppose. Shall I bring these nails and things for you?' And she gathered up the pliers and other tools, hoping Willie's father would follow her away from the coalshed before he heard the scratching just inside the door.

She went with him to the workshop and then she said goodbye and escaped before he could tell her any more about what his father used to say. She slipped behind the quince hedge into the orchard to wait for him to go inside so she could return to search for the hare but Mr Tromp tinkered about in the feedroom and then he stood by the goat-kraal and smoked his pipe and spoke to the old man Ekkies.

Rosie wandered about among the fig and pomegranate and guava trees looking for something to eat. Only the guavas were ripe and she picked one and divided it in two, inspecting it for worms. Close by,

sitting on his perch, chain dangling from his foot, was Adoonsie the baboon. Hunched, small, he gazed at her.

'Hello Adoonsie,' she said. He held out his hand like a beggar-child. She offered him the guava and he bent and snatched it. He sat very still as he ate and looked off somewhere far beyond the orchard and the farmhouse. Then he turned to Rosie, put his hand out once again and grunted. She looked into his eyes. They were dark and empty.

As she gazed at him she knew, suddenly, that the small baboon had lost his *isithunzi*. It was gone. Gone. He had lost it when they'd tied a chain around his leg. Once he was a wild thing. Now he sat on his perch begging fruit – eating whatever people gave to him. He might as well be dead.

She understood – at that moment, quite distinctly – what *isithunzi* meant. It was light in the eyes, the taste of the night, the freedom to hunt or to hide or to forage. *Isithunzi* was being able to follow the little moon or to watch the stars in quietness. How could there be *isithunzi* without hope – with a pole and a chain or a hutch and a bowl?

Rosie stood there staring at Adoonsie, knowing now what she must do. She must let the small hare go. Jacoba and the trapper had been right, after all. She could never tame him or make of him a pet. She must take him out and leave him when the moon was small so he could grow with it in brightness.

'Still here, Rosie?' said Mr Tromp, leaning over the hedge.

Rosie turned, flustered. 'I was just talking to Adoonsie,' she said.

'Don't go too close,' warned Mr Tromp. 'Man, he can bite!' Rosie glanced at Adoonsie and wondered what profit Mr Tromp could find in chaining him. 'It's late,' said Mr Tromp. 'Your Ma will be calling for you. You better go home before the Tokoloshe gets you!' And he laughed and watched her until she reached the gate.

Rosie pushed her bike slowly back along the road, wondering what to do. The wind had dropped, the sun had sunk below the ridge and already her mother would be worried if she stayed out any longer. But Rosie knew that the hare would die in the coalshed if she didn't set it free that night. There was no choice but to wait until it was dark, creep from the house when no one would discover her, fetch the hare from Willie's and go down to Kareebos to release it.

She wished Skip could come with her. He was not afraid of the dark – of jackal, *rooikat* or diviner. He would take his torch and whistle as he went along like he always did. But she couldn't even tell him with Willie there. She would have to go alone.

Her shadow bobbed over bushes and grass – flat here, standing up there against a tree trunk like a grown Rosie. She watched it walking with her and wondered if people might have an *isithunzi* too and if hers was able to protect her out there in the night.

Skip had a small, strong *isithunzi*, she was sure. And so did Oukan. Tantyi Mayekiso, it seemed to her, was all *isithunzi* – just as though he were the ghost of the diviner that had lived among the rocks where the

64

kannabos grew up. And Jacoba Pandoer? She had had one once even if she'd lost it like Adoonsie. In the end, Rosie thought, it was better to have lost it and be sad than never ever understand what *isithunzi* was – never care or know what had been missed.

8

Rosie wandered from room to room waiting for the dark. Oukan was sitting in the kitchen having tea. Rosie felt comfortable and safe near Oukan. If she could only tell him what she had to do he would understand, she knew. She watched him drink from the old white enamel mug. He gazed ahead, his eyes small and bright as though he was watching something lively and absorbing in his thoughts that no one else could reach.

When Rosie's father came up the back steps from the dairy Oukan took his hat and went away, and Rosie trailed off into the house and sat on her mother's bed and watched her as she did her hair. She wanted to burrow down into the eiderdown and close the cur-

66

tains so she could not see the night outside, so she could forget about the hare in Willie's coalshed and the lonely track leading to Karreebos.

She took the jewellery box from the drawer and tried on the bracelets and earrings, chattering brightly but not looking up in case her mother saw her face and asked her what was wrong. She wished her parents weren't going out. She did not want to be left alone in the empty room with the smell of warm water and shampoo and jasmine and no one to reassure her. She did not want to watch the car back out of the garage and drive away, its little red tail-lights getting smaller and smaller like the eyes of a springhare in the dark.

When they had gone Rosie went back to the kitchen to find Nomatse or Dan but Dan was still being scrubbed in the bathroom at the end of the house, and Skip and Willie were ferreting in the pantry for food for their midnight feast.

Willie seemed to be agitated, as though he was thinking of something and didn't want to be there. Once he asked Skip what wild hares ate and when Skip said he didn't know and talked about hunting instead, Willie didn't seem to listen but frowned and pulled at his ears in a thoughtful way.

Rosie went to the back door and looked out. The ridge behind the house loomed very black and silent. But just above it, in a sky green with the sinking light of evening, the new moon hung. Rosie gazed at it knowing what it meant. It seemed as if it might have waited for her, choosing its time to rise when she had no other choice but to free her hare.

Rosie yawned rather loudly all through supper and then she said, 'I'm so tired I'm going to bed.'

'What about the midnight feast?' mouthed Skip, glancing at Dan to see if he had understood.

'If I hear you that's fine! Don't go and wake me yourself, see?'

Skip looked at her keenly. Rosie never missed midnight feasts.

As she passed the pantry Rosie took the torch from a shelf and hid it under her shirt. She went to her room and closed the door. She took off her tackies and dropped them and the torch outside the window and pulled her nightie over her jeans. Skip and Willie burst in.

'Knock, Skip!' said Rosie primly, playing the big sister.

'Why?' said Skip, bewildered. 'Where's the torch, hey?'

'I've no idea.'

'Why you going to bed in your clothes?' said Willie, pointing to her trouser legs sticking out below her hem.

'I was getting undressed,' said Rosie, flustered.

Willie looked at her suspiciously but Rosie stared him out, her colour high.

Skip and Willie went to search elsewhere and Rosie climbed into bed. She opened her book and tried to read but after a time she switched off the light and lay listening to the sound of Nomatse's radio playing in the kitchen and Skip and Willie laughing in the room next door.

If Skip had been alone he would have been cleaning his gun or making a wire-car or reading comics and she would have called him so they could go and free the hare together.

She got out of bed and arranged the pillows to look like a body. She rolled a dark pyjama top into a ball for a head and then she took her nightie off and stuffed it under the covers. She found a shirt and jersey and climbed out of the window. She fumbled for her tackies and the torch. Then she crept along the stoep, stopped at Skip's window and peered in.

Skip sat on his bed reading. Willie was rolling marbles across the wooden floor. He was wearing Dan's dassie-skin cap and eating a stick of biltong. He gnawed at it, growling almost. It seemed to Rosie as if he was worrying the meat into his mouth.

He looked up suddenly, listening, an anxious expression on his face. Rosie shrank back. Then he glanced restlessly at Skip as though he wanted to say something but didn't know how. Rosie wondered if he was worried about the hare, if he was deciding – as she had done – what he should do with it. Perhaps Tantyi Mayekiso had been watching her the day she'd taken the hare from the shed the way she now watched Willie. Perhaps he'd seen her after all and decided she could have it.

She stood for a moment looking at Willie and thinking of these things and then she went to the feedroom and found a sack. She returned to the yard and opened the door of the rabbit-hutch. She drew out one of the sleepy white rabbits and put it in the sack. Then she

69

took her bicycle, which she had hidden near the gate, and rode away.

Rosie was not afraid on the road to Willie's farm. It was too familiar for ghosts or spirits, too well-used for jackals – for there was the shed by the bend and there was Oukan's little house and there the reservoir and the bush where she had often found the tracks of a solitary steenbok in the sand.

She could see the tall trees that grew around Willie's house – the sad cypresses and the big, pale blue-gum by the shed. She hoped Baas the bull terrier was inside and would not bark at her. She crept through the orchard, keeping as far from the house as she could. Adoonsie was not on his pole but she heard the clink of his chain as though, like a small, lonely sentinel, he had sensed her and watched her pass from some dark hiding-place.

Rosie went to the coalshed. She switched on her torch, flicking the beam through the room. Dhau sat in a corner among the coalbags. She kept the beam on his face to blind him momentarily. Then she stooped and caught him. She tipped the white rabbit gently to the floor and closed the sack over Dhau.

She went outside and shut the door. She stood breathing deeply, looking over at the house. The shutters were closed and the light was dim behind them. The windmill creaked suddenly as though its joints were settling in for the night.

Rosie went back through the orchard and down to the place where she had left her bicycle. She rode carefully, sack and hare resting in the crook of her arm.

When she reached the district road she peddled faster, afraid a car might come. She passed the siding and the shed and the house where Tant Jacoba lived. The door was open and the lights shone out, flat across the sandy ground of the yard. Rosie hurried on.

The nights are very dark on those hills. The wind comes soon after the sun has gone: a dry wind, often hot, and the bushes, which seem to have been made of stone, bend before it and the grass is shaken free. There are no people in the night. They are closed away beyond the sight of the stars. It is the time when all the hidden creatures of those koppies and the wide grey plains are about: bat-eared foxes and aardwolf with their strange, sloping haunches and shuffle gait. There are antbears, and on the ridges lynxes and jackals hunt.

'He becomes a jackal in the night,' Willie Tromp had said of Tantyi Mayekiso. 'He sucks blood any time he can get it.' Rosie glanced about fearfully. Her front tyre wobbled a little on the road. Maybe Tantyi Mayekiso had doubled back just like a jackal and lain down to wait in his tracks so the wind could pass over him and miss his scent. Then, slowly, as night came on, perhaps his eyes had changed from black to amber. Perhaps he had lured her there with the hare, hoping she would come and set it free just as he had lured the jackal and the *rooikat* with his *mutis*.

Rosie stopped. Her breath was shallow like the panting of the little hare when first she'd touched it. She peered around into the darkness, holding the hare close, her fingers resting on the sack, taking comfort

71

from its warmth. She could feel the blood surging in her ears and she clenched her teeth to keep from trembling. Nothing moved. Not even a bullfrog in the furrow croaked out his foolish song. The bush stretched black around her out towards the ridge where the bulk of the diviner's rock stood up.

Rosie went on slowly, pushing her bike towards the turning to Kareebos. And then, somewhere out across the plains, thin and far, she heard a jackal yelp. The hare seemed to cower in her arms and Rosie dropped her bike and half-ran back towards the small beacon-light of the Pandoers' house. She called softly, tapping with her fingers on the open door.

Jacoba had heard her – the timid squeak of the gate, the footsteps flitting up the path. She came through the kitchen and looked down at Rosie standing there.

'I'm going to set the hare free, 'stammered Rosie. 'It will die if I don't.'

Jacoba nodded.

'The trapper,' Rosie continued uneasily, trying to explain why she was there. 'Where is he? Do you know?'

'I have not seen him.'

'He said I must let the hare go when the moon was new and didn't have it's shadow yet.' She glanced over her shoulder. 'Do you think he's gone away?'

'Perhaps.'

'But maybe he's still there, on Kareebos . . .'

'He might be.'

'Well . . .' Rosie hesitated.

Jacoba said quietly, 'I will come with.' She closed the

door behind her and followed Rosie down the path.

They walked a little way without speaking and then Rosie said, 'Willie Tromp took my hare.'

'Willie Tromp,' said Jacoba Pandoer, as though she had never heard the name before.

'He always wanted rabbits but his Pa said', Rosie thought for a moment, 'if there's no profit, there's no point.'

'No point,' said Jacoba as though the words were something she were turning over to examine.

'I think he will be very sad when he sees I've taken it back. I think he thought we'd lost it and we wouldn't know he'd found it and he really wanted to have it as a pet like Adoonsie. Anyway,' she hurried on, 'I left one of my white rabbits for him because he likes their red eyes so much and he's not so bad. He can't help it about his Dad. And he's never heard of *isithunzi* so he wouldn't know he couldn't make it tame.'

'You cannot tame something if that is not the thing it wants,' said Jacoba.

'How do you know?' asked Rosie.

Jacoba walked on, her footsteps big and ponderous in the soft sand. 'They locked me up, once.'

Rosie could feel the pulse in her throat fluttering again. She remembered suddenly that Willie had said, 'Who'd want to live with *Boesmans* in a *stroois*? Perhaps Jacoba knew Tantyi Mayekiso. Perhaps she knew him well. Once Jacoba'd sent her to him – right there on Kareebos by herself. Perhaps they'd made a plan together, laughing in the dark about the way they'd catch her: Tantyi Mayekiso with his sing-song

73

voice and Tant Jacoba with her wayward eyes. Maybe they were both mad after all, like Willie said. Rosie stopped, ready to run. 'Why did they lock you up?' she said.

'They locked me up in the Children's Home,' said Jacoba. 'I didn't want to be there.'

'Why?'

'*Ag*, man, it was a long time ago.'

'Didn't you have a mother and a father?' said Rosie, almost accusing.

Jacoba shook her head. 'I lived with my Ouma and my Oupa there near Deelfontein. There was Koos and Anna that was staying on the farm and looking after things. There was the children Simphiwe and Nkwinki and Witbooi and Tos.'

Rosie stood just close enough to hear Jacoba's words.

'Ouma and Oupa were old. They didn't do much except staying on the stoep. *Ag*, man,' said Jacoba again, 'it was a long time ago. Ouma died first. Then Oupa. So there was nothing. Not for Koos and Anna. Not for me.'

'What happened?'

'Someone came and took me to the Children's Home in town.'

'What was it like?'

'You got long tables there to eat off and there's lots of other children. We was always fighting.' She gave a small laugh. Rosie had never seen her smile before. 'I run away one day. Just there out by the fence behind the hostel. I went to find Koos and Anna and Simphiwe

74

and Nkwinki and Witbooi and Tos, you see. It was a long way.'

'What did you eat?'

'*Veldkos*.'

'How did you know?'

'Koos was an old man. He was born in the veld. Simphiwe and Tos and me used to eat lots of things in the bush. We never went to school.'

'Is that how you knew about the hare and about *muti* and about his spirit,' said Rosie, more relieved than she dared show.

'*Ja*. Koos was really an old *Boesman*. That is what he was.'

Jacoba was silent. Rosie walked on slowly then beside her.

'I run away,' said Jacoba. 'I ran away back to my Oupa's farm. They was looking for me – all those people from the Home. I got to the farm before they found me. I went up the road. There was a old peppertree there by the turning to Foentjies place just near our gate. I stood and I looked down and I could see the *stroois* where Koos and Anna lived. I stood by the peppertrees. "Anna!" I called. "Anna!" I went down then.' Rose gazed at Jacoba expectantly. 'There was no one. They were gone.'

'What happened after that?'

'The people came in the car and took me back. Also Poen, he came too. They called him from the station at Biesiespoort. I didn't want to go with them. Not even Poen. So they locked me up.'

'Did you see them again?'

'See?'

'Koos and Anna and Tos and them.'

'No,' said Jacoba. 'No' – as if she had repeated it many times to herself. 'No. You can't live with these people. That is what they said.'

'Why?' asked Rosie hesitantly.

'*Ja,*' said Jacoba, in case she might forget, 'you can't live with these people. That is what they said.'

They turned into the road leading to Kareebos. White forms moved quietly in the dark around them. Rosie did not start. These, she knew, were goats. Even in the dark they were slow and quiet. They went on, the little beam of the torch exploring the path ahead. The hare shifted in the sack in Rosie's arms. It seemed to sense the great, dry, fragrant night outside.

They passed the first gate and the second, the third gate and the fourth where the boerboon tree grew close against the fence. They passed the shed and the old deserted house and walked towards the ridge, where the rock brooded with its plume of kannabos black against the sky. And above it, wraith-thin and bright, was the moon.

'The little moon, Dhau,' whispered Rosie. 'It is waiting there for you.'

The wind was warm and cool, in breaths. It lapped at their faces and the scent of the night was rich on the slope below the place where the diviner's spirit walked.

Rosie led Jacoba to the culvert overhung by thorns that the trapper had shown to her. She opened the sack and sat down on the sand with the hare in her arms.

She waited with Jacoba, no longer fearful of the foot-fall of a *rooikat*, the yelping of a jackal, of Tantyi Mayekiso. She looked about at the shadows of the thorntrees leaning in around her and the little moon hanging up above the ridge in a deep, clear, starry sky. Way off in a far ravine she heard a nightjar call – as though for it the dark, with all its company of stars, could hold no fear.

Rosie set down Dhau the hare and then slowly she backed away. He lay small and still. And then, as though all the scents of the night had given him his breath, he sat up straight and he raised his ears and looked about.

The nightjar called again and suddenly Dhau was gone, and Rosie peered into the dark unsure if he had ever been there. She turned and looked up at Jacoba Pandoer. Jacoba smiled and let out a breath as though she had been holding it in all that time.

They walked away, the beam of the torch bobbing over the track and the little moon hanging there above them in the sky. They went in silence, listening to the night, and when they reached the place where Rosie had left her bike Jacoba Pandoer picked it up and wheeled it with her down the road. 'I will go with you as far as your gate,' she said.

When they reached the turn-off Jacoba touched Rosie's shoulder – just a moment – and looked at her with her wayward eye as though it was important to remember something, and she said, 'Goodbye, *meisie*.'

Rosie mounted her bicycle and rode away and when

she turned to wave she could see that Jacoba Pandoer
was standing very still, watching her.

9

Skip and Willie were searching for Rosie. They had
gone to her room to call her, because Skip said she'd
never left him out of a midnight feast and, besides,
three were better than two – someone could be on
guard in case Nomatse started prowling around or Dan
woke up. Skip shook the mound of pillows in the bed
and then he switched on the light and saw the rolled
pyjamas.

Willie stared and said, 'Where's she gone?'

'Don' no,' replied Skip, puzzled.

They went through the house looking for Rosie but
they could not find her.

'D'you think she's playing a joke on us, hiding like
this?' said Willie.

'What for?' said Skip impatiently. Rosie didn't make that kind of joke.

Willie could feel the sweat pricking his upper lip. His ears were hot and he glanced at Skip to see if he had noticed. 'Skip. . . ,' he began, but then he stopped and followed Skip down the passage, picking at his ear and wondering.

Perhaps, somehow, Rosie knew he'd taken the hare. Perhaps it was she and not Oukan who had hidden it. What if she had gone to fetch it back and something had happened to her out there in the dark? And if it had, would it be his fault? Willie sniffed anxiously and rubbed his nose.

He tried not to imagine jackals lurking at the roadside waiting for Rosie. He glanced at Skip again, knowing that if Rosie had hidden the hare and if she'd gone to find it she'd have told him. Rosie always told Skip everything.

If Skip had a secret or was fooling with him, Willie could usually tell – and then, if he wouldn't say what it was, Willie could always try to punch it out of him. But looking at him – Skip, he was sure, did not know about the hare. Rosie had gone and Skip was bothered. And worried. And also cross. So, if it wasn't the hare – what was it? What else could make Rosie go out at night?

'I know!' said Willie suddenly. 'I know where she is, Skip!' He tugged at Skip's arm.

'Quiet!' hissed Skip, peering into the kitchen, where Nomatse was asleep in a chair near the stove. They crept past her and let themselves out of the back door. They ran across the yard towards the shed.

81

'Skip! Listen, man!' said Willie urgently.

'*Ja?*'

'I bet Tant Jacoba got her!'

'Are you mad?' said Skip. 'Rosie wouldn't go there in the dark!'

'There's people that make *muti* out of other people's hearts which can force you to listen to them. Maybe Tannie Jacoba's got that kind of *muti*.'

Skip didn't seem to be listening. He pushed open the door of the shed where the bicycles were kept. Rosie's was gone.

'You see!' said Willie. He began to shiver. 'Mad Jacoba got her! Maybe she put her down the borehole behind the house. There was a man that did that once.'

'Shut up, Willie!' said Skip in alarm. He started off towards the gate leading to the farm road.

'Maybe we should take the bikes,' said Willie, running after him to stop him. 'Maybe we should just go to Tant Jacoba's and say we know Rosie's there and she must give her up to us . . .'

They turned back to the shed and, as they did, they saw – just beyond the second grid – a small light waving about.

'What's that?' whispered Willie hoarsely.

'It's a light, stupid!'

Willie stared a moment and then he said, 'My Pa says that there's this huge *boomslang* that goes around at night and its got one eye that kind of glows.'

'What *boomslang*?' Skip swallowed, despite himself.

'It's as long as ten mambas put together and its eye is green.'

82

Skip said a rude word.

'S'true!' said Willie.

'Don't be a big *bangbroek*, Willie!' said Skip as bravely as he could but he dragged Willie down behind a bush just in case. They waited, listening, huddled close. Willie could feel small drops of sweat sliding down his cheek. The light came nearer and they could hear the familiar creaking of a bicycle and the sigh of the tyres in the soft sand.

'I'm sure it's Rosie!' breathed Skip as he peered through the branches of the bush. 'Look!' He could see her face every now and then as the torch-beam caught it.

Willie wiped his forehead and his nose on the sleeve of his pyjamas and then, because he didn't know what else to say to hide his relief, he pulled Skip closer and hissed, 'Let's give her a fright!' And before Skip could stop him he leapt into the track yelling, 'Waaaaaahhh! Waaaaaahhh!' and waving his arms.

Rosie almost let the bicycle fall, but then she steadied it, dismounted and said in a matter-of-fact voice, 'What're you doing running around at night, Willie? Weren't you afraid I was the Thikoloshe?'

'He's the big *boomslang* from Kommadagga!' said Skip, coming out from behind the bush. 'It's *you* who's supposed to be afraid of *him*!'

Willie looked at Rosie a moment, confused by her composure.

'Where've you been, Rosie?' said Skip. 'Where've you been, hey?'

But Rosie only laughed and said, 'Never mind!' She

gave him a small, secret pinch to be quiet and then she mounted her bike again as though it was perfectly normal for her to be peddling about in the dark.

They saw the headlights of a car way off at the turning from the district road. 'Watch out, Willie!' said Skip. 'Here comes another *boomslang!*'

Willie shoved him with his shoulder. 'You think I'm stupid, hey?' He glanced behind him. 'It's your Ma and Pa coming back!'

'We better gap it!' said Skip. 'Here Rosie, stick the bike in the ditch.'

They pulled the bicycle behind some bushes. Already Willie was clambering over the gate. Skip and Rosie followed, laughing as they ran.

'Don't forget the midnight feast,' said Willie, squeezing through Skip's window. 'We'll call you when your Ma and Pa have gone to bed.'

Rosie slipped into her room. She heard the sound of her mother's voice as she came down the hall. She flew into bed in her clothes – tackies and all. The door opened and the light from the passage fell across the floor. Rosie closed her eyes and lay quite still. Her mother stood a moment looking at her and then she went away to Dan's room. Her tread was soft and reassuring.

Rosie curled up, waiting for her father to switch off the generator, but she fell asleep long before she heard it winding down. When she awoke the house was already full of morning sounds and Dan was scuffling under Skip's bed, sharing the forgotten midnight feast with Sipho. And when Rosie's father came in from the dairy for breakfast he said rather absently, 'I wonder what Jacoba Pandoer was doing wandering about near our gate last night.'

Willie glanced at Rosie sharply.

'Maybe she was looking for the big *boomslang* from Kommadagga . . . ' began Skip.

Willie kicked at his shin.

'It had nothing to do with a *boomslang*!' interrupted Rosie. 'She was making spells to turn hares into white rabbits. Ask Willie! He knows all about it! Jacoba's got lots of secrets, hey Willie?' She smiled and then she winked at him. He stared back, red and bewildered.

'And you, Rosie,' said her mother, 'seem to have lots of secrets too!'

'Secrets?' said Rosie innocently.

'Just for instance – what were your filthy old tackies doing in your bed this morning?'

Rosie laughed and tilted her head and tried to make her eyes slide out towards their corners like Jacoba Pandoer's.

'Jacoba's secrets are hers!' she said. 'And mine are mine!'

NOTE ON THE 'WILD HARE', THE RIVERINE RABBIT

The riverine rabbit, *Bunolagus monticularis*, is one of the least known and most endangered mammals in South Africa. It was probably more widely distributed in years gone by but now it is found only in undisturbed riverine bush in certain parts of the Karoo such as the Calvinia, Sutherland, Deelfontein and Victoria West districts.

For many years scientists were undecided about whether this little creature was a rabbit or a hare. They have now established that it is a unique species, more closely allied to rabbits.

So rare is it that it has been sighted by scientists only eight or nine times since it was 'discovered' in 1903. Captain G. C. Shortridge, who was the Curator of the Kaffrarian Museum in King William's Town, spent twenty years looking for the riverine rabbit and it is said that he offered a pound sterling to anyone who could bring him a specimen. That is how it came to be known as the *'pondhaas'*. It is also named the *'vleihaas'*, while others call it *'doekvoetjie'* because of the thick fur on its feet.

But for me the most intriguing name is the 'Bushman Hare'. Could *Bunolagus monticularis* have been the hare in the old Southern San legend whose lip was split by the moon when it asked too often why its mother was dead? In answer the moon gave the message that when we die we return just as the moon does: waning, sinking and then rising again.

And how long will it be before the riverine rabbit or the 'Bushman Hare' disappears from the Karoo and slips into legend as the Southern San have done?

I have called the riverine rabbit in my story Dhau, the hare, even though I am aware that 'riverine rabbit' is scientifically correct. I have done this because it is more likely that it would be referred to as a *pondhaas*, *doekvoet* or hare in the country districts, especially by farm children. Also in the San myth, it was a hare who asked the meaning of life and death from the moon.

I have taken the liberty of moving the riverine rabbit in my story a little to the east of the places where it is known to exist at present. This is because I believe that its range used to be wider than it is now and because I could not transplant my friends 'Rosie, 'Skip' and 'Dan' from their 'natural habitat' as easily as I could transplant my half-mythical Dhau!

Marguerite Poland

Information on *Bunolagus monticularis* from Reay H. N. Smithers: *The Mammals of the Southern African Subregion*, University of Pretoria, Pretoria, 1983.

GLOSSARY

aardwolf, maned jackal

bangbroek, 'scaredy cat'

Boesman, 'Bushman', person with San features or forebears

boerboon, a tree, the 'farmer's bean'

boomslang, a poisonous tree-snake

dagbrekertjie, stone chat

doekvoet, the riverine rabbit (reference to its big feet)

gwarri, a small tree

hanslammetjie, an orphaned lamb

isithunzi, the shadow of a man, animal; spirit

jiza bird, a Karoo prinia or tinktinkie

kannabos, a Camdeboo stinkwood

kapater, castrated goat

kolhaas, scrub hare

maas, sour milk

Molo!, Greetings!

mompara, fool, idiot

msenge, kiepersol, cabbage tree

muti, medicine

mvundla, Xhosa word for a common hare

Qamata, ndiphe amandla!, God, give strength to me!

rooikat, caracal lynx

strooihuis, stroois, straw house, labourer's house

thikoloshe or tokoloshe, a hairy little mannikin from Xhosa folklore

tollie, castrated bull calf

Uyez 'ngoku, He is coming now

veldkos, food gathered from the veld or bush

witgat, the shepherd's bush